Norah Bedorah

and the
Pink Doughnut with Sprinkles

"A Groovy Grandmas Story"

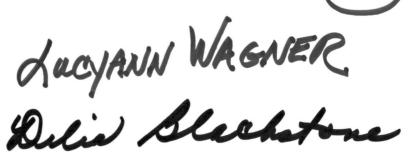

Written By Delia Blackstone & Lucyann Wagner
Illustration and artwork by Patrick Sean Langa
& Lulu Publishing

It's GROOVY to read!

ISBN: 978-1-4834-5090-2 (SC)
ISBN: 978-1-4834-5526-6 (e)

Library of Congress Control Number: 2016907851

Lulu Publishing Services rev. date: 7/13/2016

DEDICATION

The **Groovy Grandmas** dedicate this book to Nicholas, Marie Rose, Max, Brady, Tyler, Luke, Angela, Dominick, Dylan, Carter, Hayden, Lucy, and Norah, our thirteen precious grandchildren.

Our grandkids make

all our days

groovy!

Norah Bedorah
and Lucy Patoocy

Were most happy sisters

and dearest of friends.

They loved to play and have all kinds of fun.

Were they always good?
Well, that depends!

The girls had two grandmas who loved to read books,

Two grandmas as **groovy** as **groovy** could be.

Dressed up in bright sparkles and yellow tutus,

None were more fun than Grandmom and DeeDee!

The grandmas got Norah and Lucy one day

For a special playtime and sleepover date.

They had puppet shows and played dress-up,

Watched girlie movies and stayed up late.

When morning came, the grandmas called,

"Get up, sleepyheads. It's time to eat.

Good, healthy fruit to make you strong,

One pink doughnut with sprinkles, a special treat!"

Lucy Patoocy ate really fast,

Cleaned her plate and began to sing,

"Yummy, yummy in my tummy.

Thank you, Grandmas, for everything!"

But Norah Bedorah said, "NO, NOT ME!"

She folded her arms and made a **mean** face.

"**Lots** of pink doughnuts with sprinkles

but none of the fruit,

That's **all** I want at my grandmas' place!"

"Norah Bedorah," said the Groovy Grandmas.

"You can have a pink doughnut, but only just **one**!

You must listen to us and be a good girl.

When you are done, we will go have some fun."

Norah folded her arms and made a **mean** face.

"No fruit for me. I don't like it, you see!"

She threw down her plate and stuck out her tongue.

"I want my own way!

This is how it must be!"

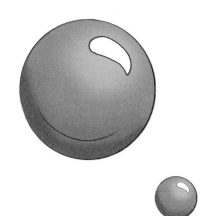

"Well, Norah Bedorah," said Lucy Patoocy,

"Let's think of something that you can do

To wow the grandmas and make them say,

'Lots of pink doughnuts with sprinkles for you!'"

"I've got it," said Norah. "I know what I'll do.

I'll blow a **gigantic** bubble-gum bubble.

It will make our grandmas laugh and clap.

I'll get **lots** of doughnuts without any trouble!"

Norah's bubble was something to see!

She floated right up to the bright blue sky.

The grandmas were really frightened for her.

They hoped she'd come back as they waved good-bye.

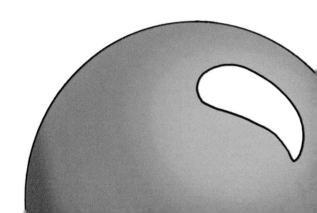

The big bubble-gum bubble finally did **burst**.

"I want **lots** of doughnuts, maybe a **TON**!"

Norah yelled as she fell in a huge pile of leaves.

The grandmas weren't sure she deserved even **one**!

"Eating **lots** of doughnuts," the grandmas said,

"Could turn you into a doughnut, it's true!

We would have to roll you all around town.

Norah, you really just wouldn't be **YOU!**"

Norah pictured herself so round and pink

With gooey pink icing stuck in her hair.

There'd be **lots** of sprinkles dotting her cheeks,

And kids around her would stop and stare.

"Oh, no!" Norah exclaimed. "That can't be **me**!

I could **never, ever** go out to play.

And **lots** of doughnuts could make me sick.

I'm learning …

I can't **always** have my own way!"

"So, Lucy," said Norah, "please listen to me.

I need to think of a really good way

To show that I'm sorry and want to behave.

Oh, wait, I've got it! Let's try this today."

"Our **Groovy Grandmas** are so much fun.

Let's write for them a **snazzy** song.

It will be **groovy** as **groovy** can be,

One they'll remember all their lives long."

The girls sang their song as the grandmas cheered.

They wore frilly dresses with jewels and a crown.

The grandmas both twirled in their tutus and bows,

And they all "**got their groove on**" at the

Very ...

Best ...

Party ...

In ...

Town!

Then Norah Bedorah ate

NE

Pink Doughnut with Sprinkles

And even some fruit.

The *GROOVY GRANDMAS* Song

Written by Norah Bedorah and Lucy Patoocy

They're the *Groovy Grandmas*, coming to town!

They're the *Groovy Grandmas*, clowning around.

They're the *Groovy Grandmas*, getting things done.

They're the *Groovy Grandmas*, having some fun.

Get your groove on, Granny! Get your groove on!

Get your groove on, Granny! Get your groove on!

They're the *Groovy Grandmas*, going to school.

They're the *Groovy Grandmas*, thinking kids are cool.

They're the *Groovy Grandmas*, reading lots of books.

They're the *Groovy Grandmas*, getting funny looks.

Get your groove on, Granny! Get your groove on!

Get your groove on, Granny! Get your groove on!

Dee Dee, Norah Bedorah, Grandmom, Lucy Patoocy,

It's Fun to be Groovy!

Delia Blackstone (DeeDee) and Lucyann Wagner (Grandmom) are the Groovy Grandmas! Residing in the Atlanta area, they are best of friends and love playing with their grandchildren, acting silly, and laughing a lot! They share a love of children and of books, and this encouraged them to try their hand at writing their own book. We hope you enjoy reading it as much as they did creating it.